The Toot Fairy

Written by Janet R. Adams

Chasing Fireflies

The Toot Fairy by Janet Adams
Published by Chasing Fireflies Publishing, LLC
Oklahoma City, Oklahoma
First published 2021

Primary editor: Lisa Davis
Illustrator: Daniel Wlodarski
Publishing and Design Services: Melinda Martin
Text and illustrations © 2021 Chasing Fireflies Publishing, LLC

For more information or permissions, visit www.JanetRAdams.com

ISBN: 978-1-953499-00-4 (Hardback)
ISBN: 978-1-953499-01-1 (Paperback)
ISBN: 978-1-953499-02-8 (MOBI e-book)

Library of Congress Number (LCN): 2020925724

The Toot Fairy

This book is dedicated to my children.

To the parents and adults reading this book:
I never envisioned writing a book with any form of potty humor in it . . .
until I had my own kids. I love to hear their infectious laughs.
There is nothing better! I hope this book helps you laugh
with the precious children you have in your life.

Thank you for supporting an independent author. If you enjoyed this book,
please help spread the word and consider submitting an honest review of this book.

—Janet

I'm sure you've heard of
the Tooth Fairy,
but have you ever heard of
the Toot Fairy?

I bet she has
visited you today.

It's not the
most glamorous gig.

While the Tooth Fairy
delivers money for lost teeth,

the Toot Fairy's presents are...
less pleasant.

The Toot Fairy flies around the world, delivering toots to everyone and their dog.

Even the President of the United States . . .
and the President's dog.

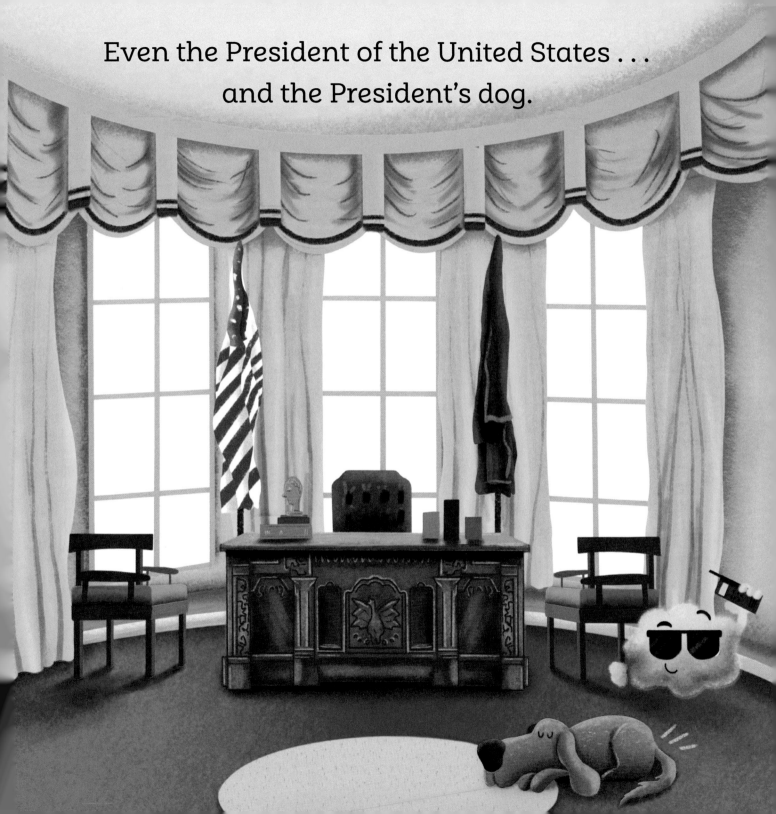

The **Toot Fairy** even has a pet toot.
His name is Gassy Gus,
but she calls him Gus for short.

If you had a pet toot,
what would you name it?

The **Toot Fairy** was almost called
the Flatulence Fairy,
and some of her friends call her
Tinker Smell.

There are just so many ways to say fart!
Can you think of any others?

She harvests baby toots
from her gassy garden.

She has to be careful not to overfeed the toots
or they can become extra stinky!

There are lots of toots
that she has to grow:

Quiet ones,

loud ones,

sneaky ones,

super smelly ones,

and the silent but deadly kind.

There is even a fart that can
follow you from room to room!
That's called the follow-me-fart.

She also delivers toots under water.
They don't smell,
but the air bubbles
give you away!

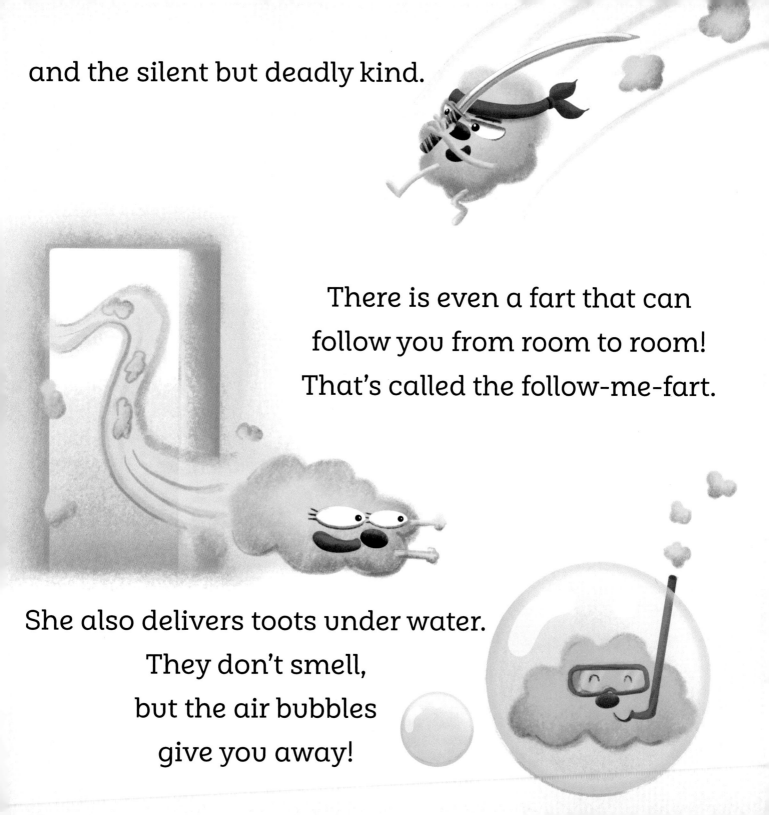

Sometimes her deliveries have pretty bad timing.
Like when the **Toot Fairy** delivered a toot
to a teacher right in the middle of class.

A little boy on the front row laughed so hard that the **Toot Fairy** visited him next.

She gets to travel to lots of
cool places all over the world every day.

One of her favorite places to visit is the grassy (or should I say gassy?) plains of Africa.

She has even been known to deliver toots to lions right when they are trying to sneak up on a zebra. That's the real reason the hyenas are laughing.

And, if you think Santa Claus
is busy on Christmas night,
you should see the Toot Fairy
on Taco Tuesday.

People eat a lot of beans
on Taco Tuesdays,
and beans keep the Toot Fairy
VERY busy!

The Tooth Fairy, on the other hand,
only gets to visit someone when they are sleeping.
One night the Toot Fairy
interrupted the Tooth Fairy's delivery
by sending her several loud toots.
It's really lucky the little girl didn't wake up
and catch them both!

But do you think
the **Toot Fairy** toots?
No, never!

She saves her best toots
just for you (and the Tooth Fairy).

And in case you're wondering,
the Tooth Fairy *did* get even
with the **Toot Fairy**.

The next time
your booty backfires,
remember you just had a visit
from the **Toot Fairy**.

Tootles!

The Toot Fairy's
Favorite Jokes

Q. **What does the Toot Fairy call her godmother?**
A. Her fairy fartmother.

Q. **What is the Toot Fairy's favorite ice cream?**
A. Tooty fruity!

Q. **What is 20 times toot?**
A. Farty!

Q. **What do you call someone who doesn't toot in front of other people?**
A. A private tooter.

Q. **Why is Jupiter the Toot Fairy's favorite planet?**
A. Because it's a gassy planet.

Q. **How does a clown's toot smell?**
A. Funny.

Q. **Why did the Toot Fairy stop telling fart jokes?**
A. Everyone said they stink!

Made in the USA
Middletown, DE
12 November 2021